CHALLENGING COLORING

A BOOK FULL OF CREATIVE COLORING

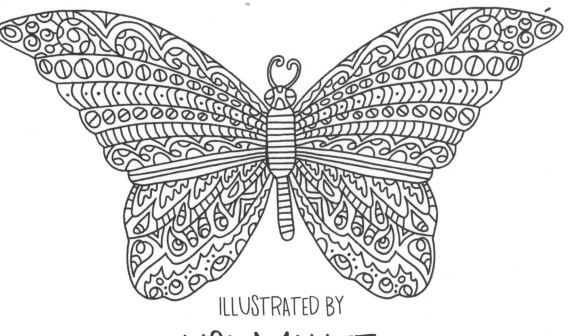

ILLUSTRATED BY

LISA MALLET

WITH ADDITIONAL DRAWINGS BY

PETRA LUKOVICSOVÁ,
MARC PARCHOW & JORGE MATEUS

BARRON'S

First edition for North America published in 2016 by
Barron's Educational Series, Inc.
First published in the U.K. by iSeek Ltd under the title, *Complicated Colouring*
This book was created and produced by iSeek Ltd
Designed by Anton Poitier and Ben Potter
Illustrated by Lisa Mallet, with additional drawings by Petra Lukovicsová, Marc Parchow,
and Jorge Mateus
Copyright ©2015 by iSeek Ltd

All inquiries should be addressed to:
Barron's Educational Series, Inc.
250 Wireless Boulevard
Hauppauge, New York 11788
www.barronseduc.com

ISBN: 978-1-4380-0780-9

Date of Manufacture: January 2016

Manufactured by: Zhong Tian Colour Printing Co., Ltd., Panyu, China

Printed in China
9 8 7 6 5 4 3

LET'S GET COLORING

This book is jam packed with amazing pictures to color. You can use either felt-tip pens or colored pencils, depending on the effect you like best. There are over 90 drawings in this book, so take your time and relax!

Felt-tip pens

Choose your favorite colors. It's a good idea to use a limited number of colors in each drawing—perhaps six to eight colors—to get a good effect.

Less complicated!

You could decide to color in only part of the picture, leaving the rest untouched. This is really effective, especially if you choose a limited range of colors.

Perforated pages

Each page in this book is perforated so that you can detach the page. Tear the pages out carefully to avoid ripping the paper. Bend the page back along the perforation and it will come out more easily.

Colored pencils

Lay out all your favorite colors and choose a set that you like. You could choose shades of one or two colors to create an interesting effect, or mix them up and use multi-colors for your drawing.

Color the outline?

All the lines in this book are gray. If you would like a black outline, trace over the lines in the printed picture with a fine black pen.

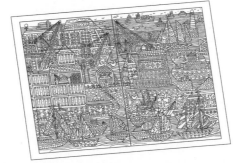

Side by side

Some of the drawings will form a scene if you detach the left page and match it up to the outside margin of the right page, placing them side by side. Cut the left-hand page along the edge of the frame with scissors, then glue it to the right-hand page to make a big scene.

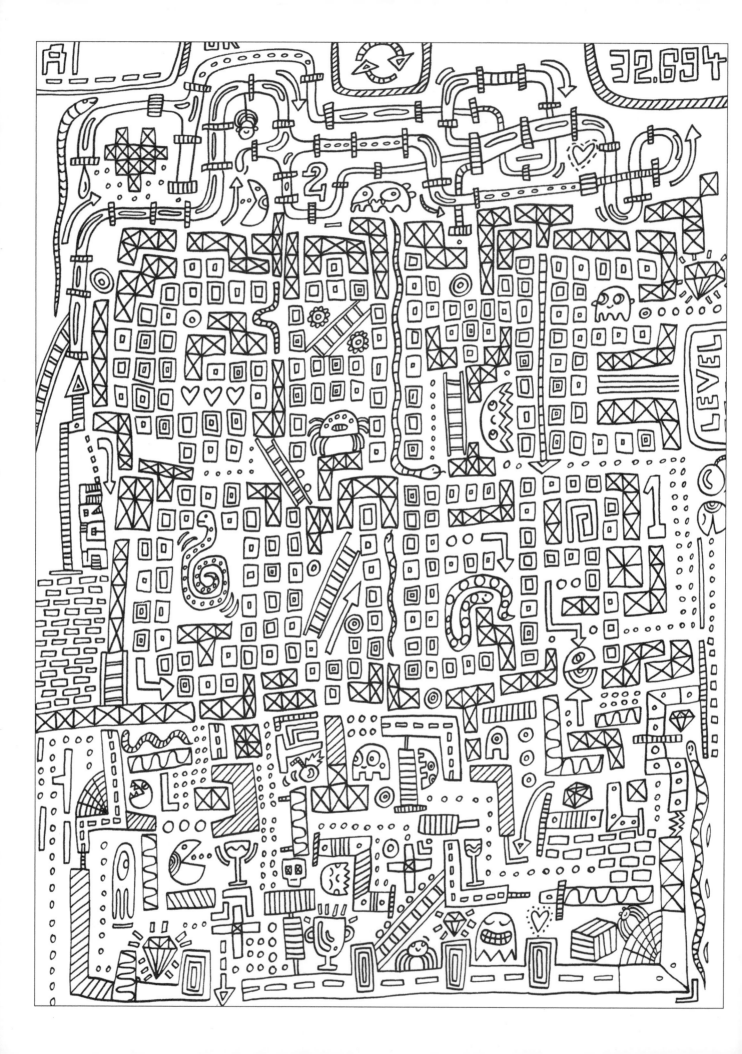

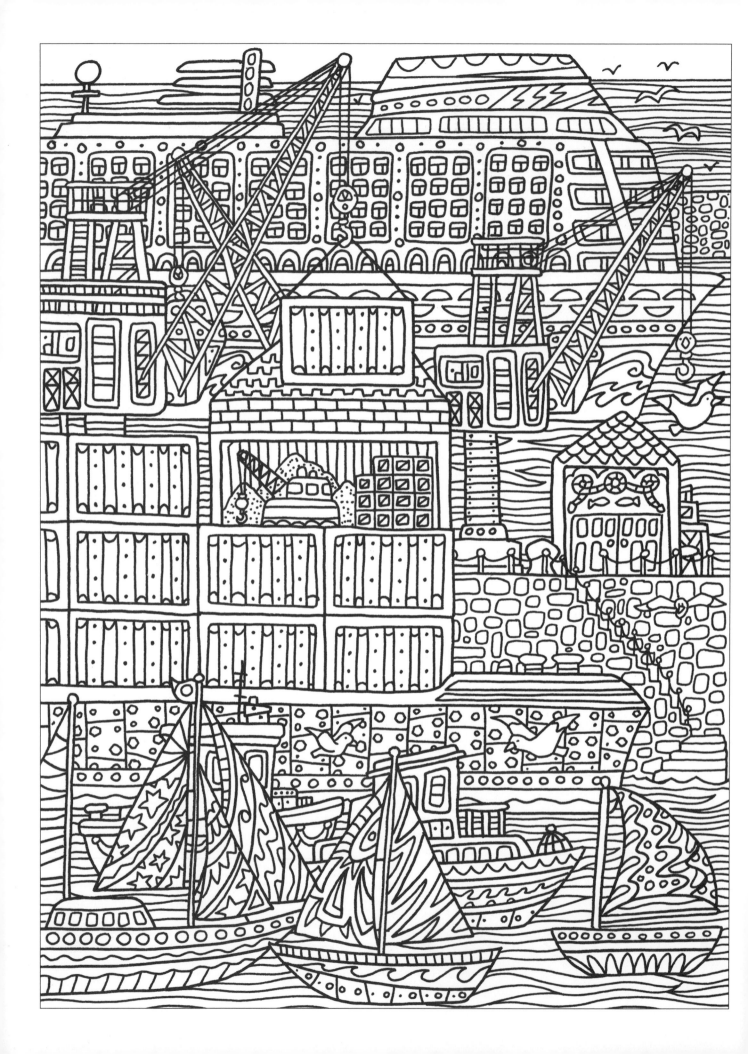

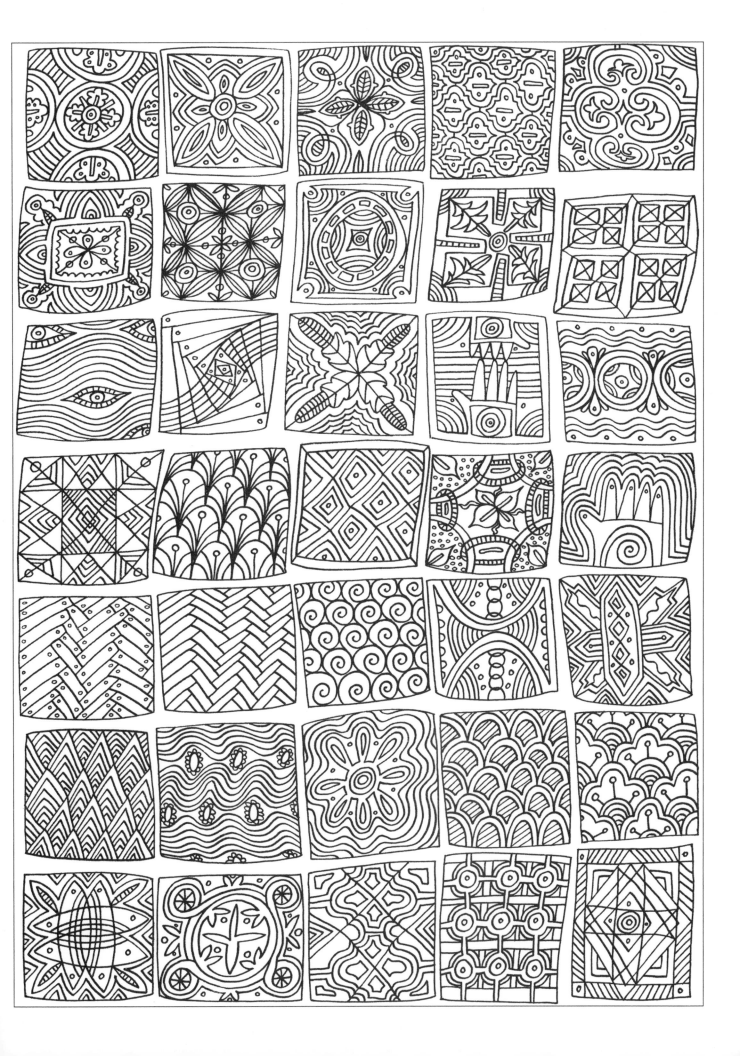

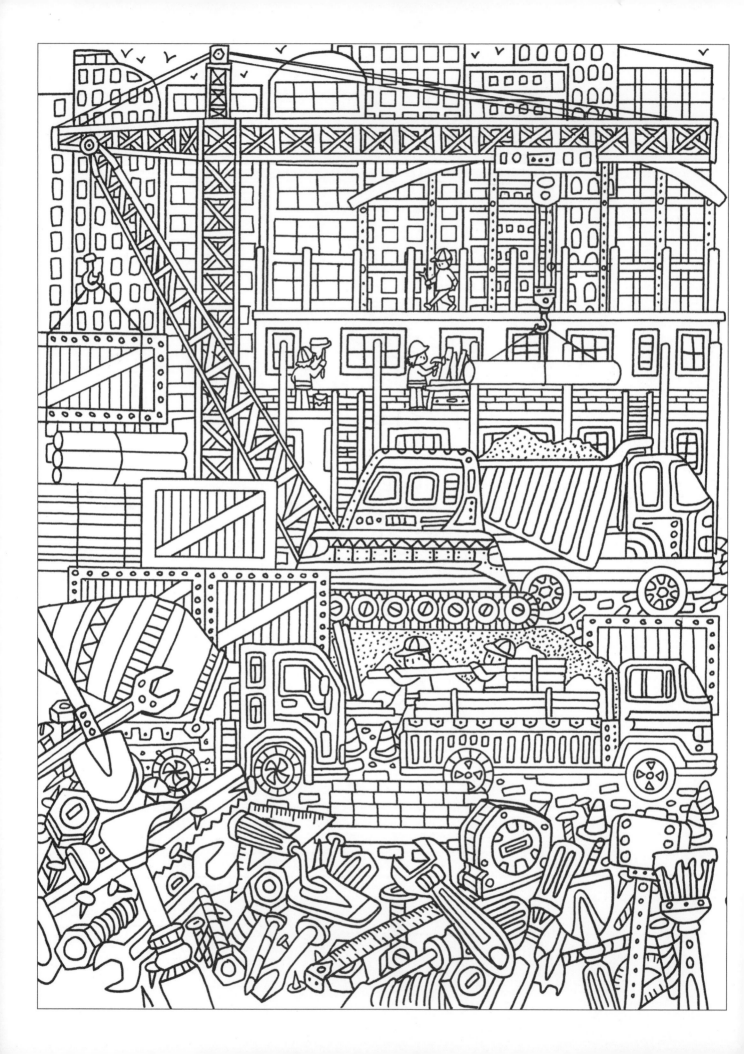

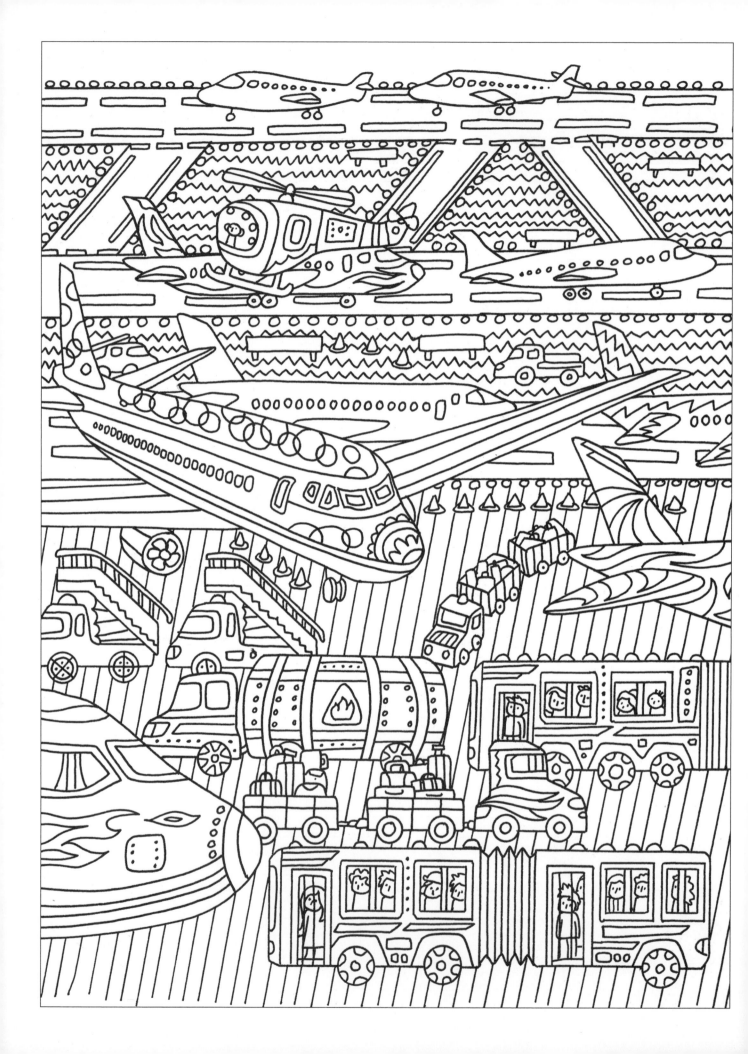

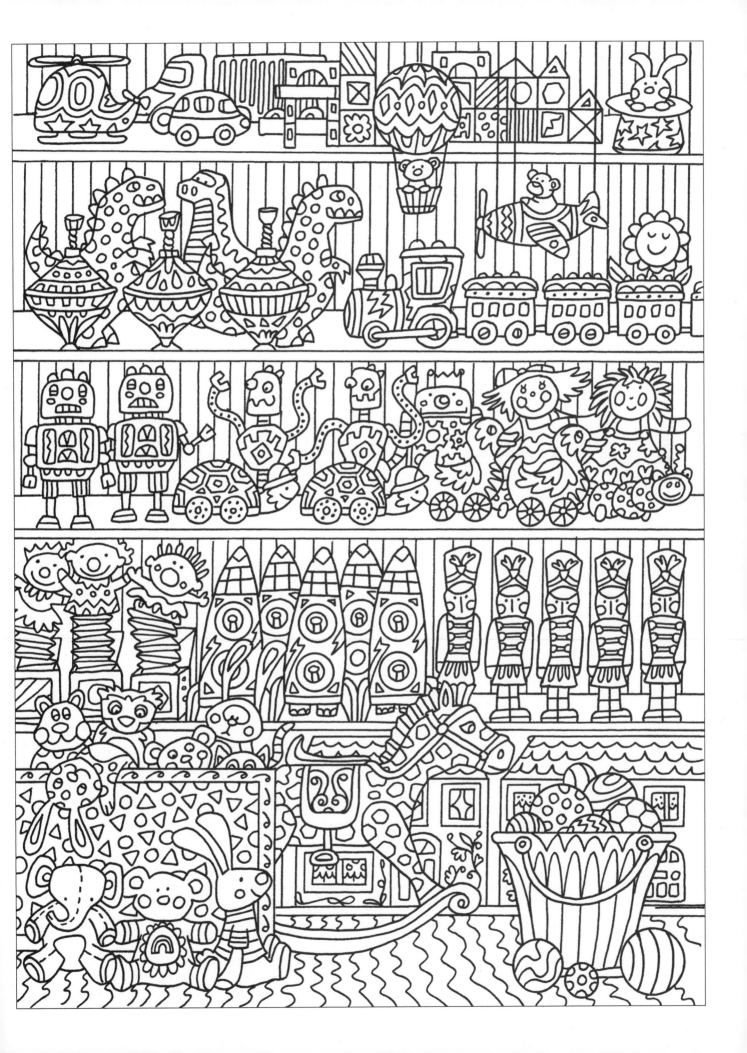

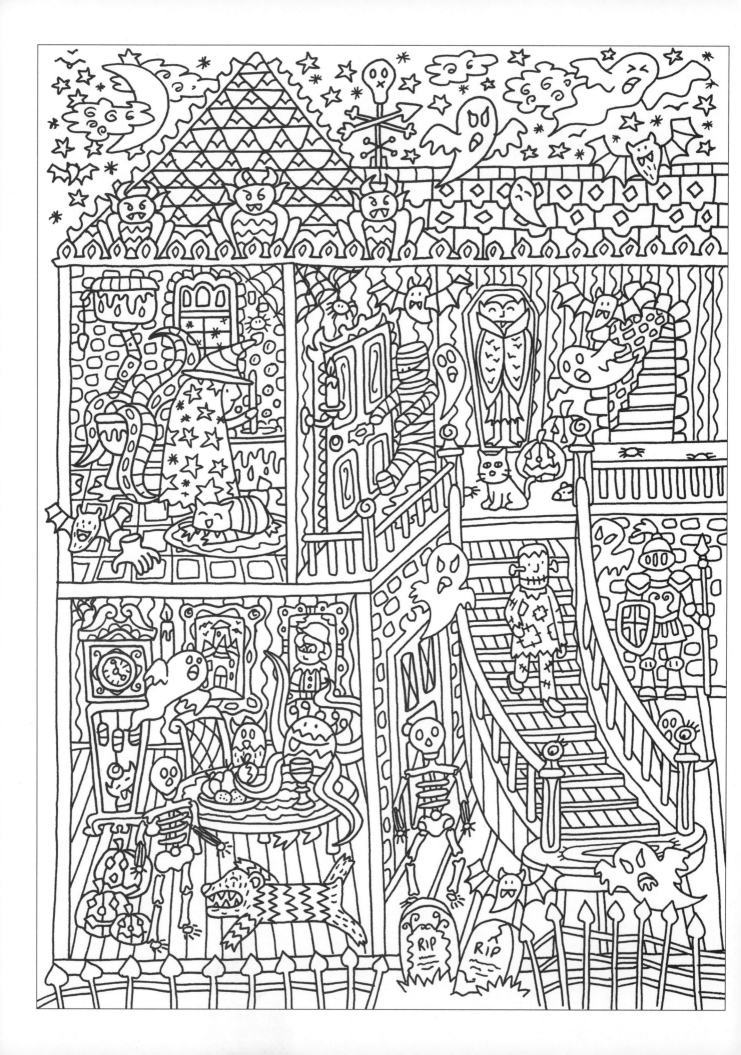